Brothers Christian

Easy Steps

Brothers Christian

Easy Steps

ISBN/EAN: 9783337300821

Printed in Europe, USA, Canada, Australia, Japan

Cover: Foto ©Andreas Hilbeck / pixelio.de

More available books at **www.hansebooks.com**

CHRISTIAN BROTHERS'

NEW SERIES.

EASY STEPS.

LA SALLE BUREAU OF SUPPLIES,
50 SECOND STREET,
NEW YORK.

CONTENTS

Lessons in verse are indicated by a *

CONTENTS.

INTRODUCTION.

The " Easy Steps " is intended to form a con-
necting link, of the most appropriate kind, be-
tween the Primer and the Elementary Reader.

The lessons have been carefully chosen. A
double end has been kept in view. It is sought to
furnish the child with a number of purely English
words, placed in such sentences as will best
show their proper use. While leading the child
from one stage of difficulty to another, his mind
is interested and stored with useful information,
pleasantly given.

It will be remarked by many that the first
lessons in the Elementary Reader are not more
difficult than those in the Easy Steps. Teachers
who will bear the object of this Series in mind,
will easily understand the compiler's motive.
The Primer and Easy Steps simply teach the
very first stages of reading. The child is not re-
quired to answer any direct question ; but is
solely occupied in word-building, pronunciation,
and acquiring a proper tone,

An important element of difficulty has been eliminated in Easy Steps. All words of two or more syllables are divided.

In a few cases, the lessons may appear rather lengthy. A special object is aimed at in this arrangement. A power of prolonged attention is developed, which is absolutely necessary to carry out the plan of the remaining numbers of the Series.

The teacher is referred, for other suggestions and directions, to the work * written to facilitate the proper use of this and the other Readers.

* Hints.

THE NOBLE HORSE.

gen-tle · trust-ed be-fore

fa-ther no-ble weak

ONE day an ox met a horse with
a lit-tle boy on his back. "Oh,
shame on you!" said the ox, "to let

a lit-tle boy ride you, and lead you
a-bout.   I would show him that he
was not so strong as I am."

But the horse held up his head,
and bent his fine neck, and said:

"No, I am proud to be gen-tle to
this weak lit-tle boy.   It would be
ver-y mean of me to hurt a hair of
his head.   As he is not so strong as
I, I am glad to give him a ride this
fine day.   When I have ta-ken him
where he wants to go, I shall bring
him back to his fa-ther, who trust-ed
me with him."

And so the no-ble horse went on
just as gen-tly as he had done be-fore.

And I said to my-self: "That is
like some no-ble boys I have seen,
who love to do kind acts to those
who are small and weak, and would
scorn to do them an-y harm."

THE GOAT.

goat	dyed	beards
crag	shag-gy	graze

I HAVE just seen a goat and her two lit-tle kids. They are not at all wild, but will come if you call them.

The kids are as fond of play as a lamb. They will leap o-ver the back of the old goat as she lies on the ground.

The goat is ver-y sure-foot-ed. It can climb high rocks, and leap from crag to crag.

The goat's hair is not at all like the wool of the sheep. In some lands it grows fine, and long, and soft as silk. It is cut off, and dyed, and made in-to rich, bright cloth.

All parts of the goat are of use to us. We drink its milk, eat its flesh, and make its skin in-to leath-er.

We of-ten see goats in this land, and there are a great man-y in oth-er parts of the world.

With their long horns, shag-gy

beaɪds, and rough coats, they look
ver-y pret-ty as they graze on the
hill-side, or stand on the high rocks.

———o———

THE BEE AND THE DOVE.

thirs-ty   thrown   de-serves
car-ried   un-hurt   helped

ONE hot day a bee, who had been
work-ing ver-y hard, and was
ver-y thirs-ty, went to drink some wa-
ter by the side of a riv-er.

But the riv-er car-ried her a-way,
and she would have been drowned, if
a dove, who had seen her strug-gles,
had not thrown a leaf to her.

The bee got on the leaf, and, as
soon as her wings were dry, she was
a-ble to fly a-way.

Not long af-ter, the dove was sit-
ting on a tree, when a man came by

with a gun.   See-ing the dove, he was a-bout to shoot it with his gun, but just at that mo-ment the bee stung him on the hand.

This made him miss his aim, and the dove was a-ble to fly a-way un-hurt.

One good turn de-serves an-oth-er. The dove helped the bee, and now the bee helped the dove.

———o———

THE TOWER.

tow-er	grubs	rush-es
i-vy	roots	riv-er

I THINK this tow-er with the i-vy on it, and the birds in the air, and the tall trees, and the flags in the riv-er, look ver-y pret-ty.

Can they be crows that live in the

tow-er? No; for crows have their
nests in trees.

They must be daws, for THEY have
heir nests in tow-ers.

Daws are like crows, but they are
not so large, and have gray on the
top of their heads.

They live on worms and grubs,

and on roots, and seeds, and the like.

Flags and rush es grow in riv-ers, or on the low, wet banks, near the wa-ter.

If I lived near a riv-er I would have a boat, and row it. I would get a hook, and a line, and a rod, and would fish.

———o———

FUN IN THE COUNTRY.

peb-bles   shin-ing   swim-ming
bot-tom   sis-ter   scales

HOW I should like to be with th it boy and girl! The bright wa-ter be-low, with the peb-bles at the bot-tom; the green grass, and the flow-ers at the sides; the flags in the wa-ter; the trees be-hind; the birds in the sky; the light shin-ing on all

things, and the soft air kiss-ing my
face, would be so fresh.

Then the bridge it-self is so pret-
ty. The boy can see his face in the
wa-ter be-low, I dare say.

His sis-ter is at the one end, and
he is call-ing her, I think, to see what
he has just seen in the wa-ter. Per-

haps it was a fish swim-ming, with its **pret-ty** scales, and its fins, and its tail.

See, he holds out his arm to get her to step to him.

———o———

FUN IN THE COUNTRY.

PART II.

nar-row   duck-lings   branch-es
wid-er   hatch   bram-bles

THIS stream is ver-y nar-row just here, but I dare say it grows wid-er as it flows on, till it is a wide riv-er with ships on it.

The lit-tle boy could wade it here, and per-haps he has wad-ed in it, and tried to catch the small fish with his hands.

The bridge is made of a plank

with some poles at the side, for a fence, to keep the boy and girl from fall-ing in-to the wa-ter.

How the birds will sing in the trees, and the larks in the air, in the bright spring days, at such a spot. Then, in sum-mer, the flow-ers will be so sweet.

There is no road, but just a path, so there will be no noise to make the birds fly a-way.

I dare say the lit-tle boy and his sis-ter will be sing-ing a song for ver-y joy, in such a place.

How I wish the boys and girls, who live in the streets of large cit-ies, and nev-er see the green grass, nor lis-ten to the song of the birds, could be in such a sweet spot now and then! It makes a boy or a girl well and strong to live in the o-pen air.

If there be a pond close by, the old duck will be sure to take her duck-lings to such a place.

I think I can see how she would wad-dle be-fore them, and swim off in-to the bright wa-ter, with all the lit-tle puffs of down swim-ming be-hind her.

The hen would not take her chicks there, for hens can-not swim. If a hen hatch ducks' eggs, the lit-tle ducks go off and swim when they can, but the hen stands on a stone, and clucks in her fright. Don't be a-fraid, hen; the duck-lings will not drown.

See how the stems of the trees bend over the wa-ter. The bank is so soft that they bend to the side, as they now are.

What a fine place these bend-ing branch-es must be for nuts.

Wild flow-ers of all kinds climb up these branch-es, or blow a-mong the grass be-low.

———o———

THE WIDOW'S MITE.

mon-ey   per-sons   pen-ny
tem-ple   wid-ow   beg-gar

A VER-Y nice thing in the life of our Lord is told a-bout the Wid-ow's Mite.   A mite was a ver-y small piece of mon-ey a-mong the Jews.   Now, all the Jews used to put mon-ey in the box in the tem-ple. The rich Jews gave large sums, and were ver-y proud, some-times, of what they gave.

One day Je-sus was in the tem-ple, and man-y per-sons were put-ting mon-ey in the box.   Je-sus looked at

THE WIDOW'S MITE.

them in si-lence for some time.
Then, turn-ing a-bout, he said to
those who were near him: "Have
you seen that poor wid-ow who has
just put her mite in-to the mon-ey
box? Let me tell you, she has done
more than an-y one else to-day. The
oth-ers have giv-en some-thing, but
have kept plen-ty for them-selves.
This poor wid-ow has giv-en from the
few pence she has in the world."

This sto-ry must please lit-tle chil-
dren great-ly. If we can-not give
much to the poor, we must do what
we can. A pen-ny giv-en by a poor
lit-tle boy or girl to a beg-gar may be
more pleas-ing to God than a large
sum of mon-ey giv-en by a rich per-
son. When we do the best we can,
God is al-ways pleas-ed. God loves
the cheer-ful giv-er. E-ven a cup of

cold wa-ter giv-en for his sake will have its re-ward. I will al-ways try to be ver-y kind to the poor.

———o———

LITTLE BIRDS AND CRUEL BOYS.

warm   guard   brood
crept   cry-ing   mourned

A LIT-TLE bird built a warm nest in a tree,
And in it laid blue eggs, one, two, and three,
And then ver-y glad and pleased was she.

But af-ter a while, just how long I can't tell,
The lit-tle ones crept, one by one, from the shell;
And their moth-er was pleased, for she loved them all well.

She spread her soft wings on them
all the day long,

I'o warm and to guard them, hei
love was so strong;
And her mate sat be-side her, and
sang her a song.

One day the young birds were all
cry-ing for food,
So off flew their moth-er a-way from
her brood;
And up came some boys, both wick-
ed and rude.

So the warm nest they pulled down
a-way from the tree;
And the lit-tle ones cried, but they
could not get free;
So at last they all died a-way, one,
two and three.

But when back to the nest the poor
moth-er did fly,
Oh, then she set up a most heart
break-ing cry!
She mourned a long while, and lay
down to die!

ABOUT HOUSES.

prop   panes   chim-neys
shade   hin-ges slope

HOUS-ES long a-go were like these. They stand with the end, or ga-ble, to the road. They were, in part, of wood. Posts of wood prop

up the front, so as to make a nice o-pen shade be-low.

Then there is a frame of wood up to the top, for parts of it are seen on the out-side.

The win-dows are of a strange shape, and if you could see them, the panes of glass are ver-y small, and the sash-es o-pen in the mid-dle, on hin-ges.

See how tall the chim-neys are, and how steep the slope of the roofs You may be sure they have not slates, as some of our roofs have.

———o———

ABOUT HOUSES.

PART II.

tiles   spar-rows   grass
thatch fence   wheels

THEY may have tiles, for old hous-es of-ten are tiled; or per-haps they have thatch on them.

Thatch is made of straw, and keeps the house ver-y warm in win-ter; but the spar-rows make holes in it in spring, for their nests, and the air and the wet soon rot it.

The win-dows on the roof have a strange shape.

I can see flow-ers and trees. See if you can.

The grass in the road tells that it is not in a cit-y or town, for the feet of men, and the wheels, and the hoofs of hors-es, will not let grass rise in cit-y streets.

———o———

TREES, HOW THEY LIVE.

frail   snapped   crows
twig   chirp   fee-ble

THE tall-est tree was, at first, a frail twig, which a boy could have snapped in play. But time has made it what it is. Birds chirp in it; crows have nests in it; the wind sings in it; the sun makes it green, and in win-ter it grows bare.

Men do not live long, but a tree has a long life. When the sun comes back af-ter win-ter, the tree grows green and gay, but men grow old and fee-ble. The tree is not so high as the tow-er, but it seems high-er, for the tow-er is far off.

Our good or bad hab-its are at first like the twig, weak, and brok-en with ease, but when old they are hard to change. We should then try while young to form on-ly good hab-its.

————o————

QUAILS AND YOUNG.

quails　be-hind　fun-ny
meek　blade　rogue

MR. Quail and Mrs. Quail, and all the lit-tle quails,
Safe at home in soft brown coats and ver-y wee-wee tails;

Fa-ther watch-ing from the wall,
  moth-er look-ing meek,
While the young-sters—sev-en in all
  —play at hide and seek.

"Where is Ti-ny?" "Let us hunt."
  "Not on moth-er's back."
"Not be-hind this blade of grass." "Is
  he down this crack?"
"Per-haps he is—he's ver-y small—
  quite a lit-tle thing."
"There he is, the fun-ny rogue, un-
  der moth-er's wing."

THE FOX AND THE STORK.

stork   sor-ry   bot-tle

lapped   plen-ty   dealt

ONE day the fox asked the stork to din-ner. The fox is a fun-ny fel-low, and he wished to play a trick

on the stork. So when the stork came, she found noth-ing on the ta-ble but soup, in wide, shal-low dishes, so that she could on-ly dip in the end of her long bill, and could not eat an-y thing. The fox lapped it up quick-ly, now and then ask-ing the stork how she liked her din-ner, hop-ing that it was to her mind, but say-ing that he was sor-ry to see her eat so lit-tle. The stork knew that he was mak-ing fun of her; but she said nothing.

Some days af-ter, the stork, in her turn, asked the fox to dine with her. Sly as he was, he did not ex-pect to be paid back in his own coin; so he went. When din-ner was served, he was much vexed to see noth-ing but some meat, cut ver-y small, and placed in a big bot-tle, the neck of which was ver-y long and nar-row. The stork, put-ting in her long bill, could help her-self to plen-ty of it; but the fox could on-ly lick the out-side of the bot-tle. The fox asked if that was all the din-ner. "Oh yes," said the stork; "I am glad to see you are so hun-gry; I hope you will make as good a din-ner at my ta-ble as I did at yours the oth-er day." The fox felt an-gry at first; but had at last to own that he had been right-ly dealt with. He felt that, if he did not like to have a joke played up-on him-self, he should not have played one up-on the stork.

We should nev-er do to oth-ers what we would not like them to do to us.

———————

HOW HE WAS CAUGHT.

i-dle	mas-ter	faults
youth	con-duct	oth-ers

"WHEN I was a boy at school,' said an old man, "I was of-ten ver-y i-dle. E-ven dur-ing les-sons I used to play with oth-er

boys as i-dle as my-self. Of course
we tried to hide this from the mas-
ter, but one day we were fair-ly
caught.

" 'Boys,' said he, ' you must not be
i-dle; you must at-tend to your books.
You do not know what you lose by
be-ing i-dle now. Youth is the time
to learn. An-y one of you who sees
a boy look-ing off his book will please
come and tell me.'

" ' Ah,' thought I to my-self, 'there
is Joe Smith, whom I don't like;
I'll watch him, and if I see him look
off his book, I'll tell.' Not ver-y
long af-ter I saw Joe look off his book,
and I at once marched up and told
the mas-ter.

" 'Indeed,' said he; 'how do you
know he was i-dle?'—' Please, sir,'
said I, 'I saw him.'—'Oh, you did.

did you; and were your eyes on your book when you saw him?'

" I was fair-ly caught; the oth-er boys laughed, and I hung my head, while the mas-ter smiled. I nev-er watched for i-dle boys again."

If we watch o-ver our own con-duct, and al-ways do our own du-ty, we shall have no time to watch for faults in oth-ers.

----o----

THE BIRD'S NEST.

| neat-ly | wool | sweet-ly |
| taught | harsh-ly | months |

HAVE you ev-er looked at a bird's nest? See how well and neat-ly it is built. God taught the birds to do this. He taught them to get the moss, the hay, and the wool, with

which their pret-ty lit-tle nest is made,
and he gave them skill to build it so
neat-ly. Will he then not much
more teach lit-tle chil-dren to love
him, and to be wise and good?

Some boys, in-stead of learn-ing
an-y good les-sons from birds, on-ly
treat them harsh-ly. Do not rob
birds of their eggs or their young.
If you ev-er see a pret-ty nest, do not
touch the eggs: they will soon pro-
duce lit-tle birds, and per-haps you
will hear them sing ver-y sweet-ly in
a few months.

Christ tells us to be-hold the birds
of the air, and by means of them he
teach-es us to put our trust in God.
He who takes so much care of lit-tle
birds will not for-get good boys and
girls.

JESUS AMONG THE JEWS.

JESUS AMONG THE JEWS

di-vine	ques-tions	buy-ing
for-get	pict-ure	thieves

THE most sa-cred book in the world is called THE HO-LY BI BLE. In the last part of this sa-cred vol-ume we are told man-y things of our di-vine Lord.

Je-sus was ev-er kind, and ev-er just. He knew when peo-ple did not de-serve to be treat-ed kind-ly, and then he told them so.

In man-y pla-ces in the Ho-ly Bi-ble we read how Je-sus was dis-pleased with the hard-heart-ed peo ple who did not o-bey his law. He told them that they would suf-fer for their pride, and al-so for the man-y bad things they kept hid-den in their hearts.

Dear chil-dren, do not for-get that Je-sus is God. He could see in-to the hearts of all those per-sons who came a-bout him. Some-times these wick-ed men asked Je-sus hard ques-tions to catch him. He then re-plied: "Wick-ed peo-ple! why do you think e-vil in your hearts?"

When we wish to do bad things, it is a sin, for sin is an-y wil-ful thought, word or deed a-gainst the law of God.

In this pict-ure Je-sus is com-ing out of the tem-ple. See that proud man in front. He has a bag of mon-ey, and has been driv-en out of the tem-ple be-cause he was buy-ing and sell-ing things in God's ho-ly house. "My house," said the meek and hum-ble Je-sus, "is a house of pray-er, but you have made it a den of thieves."

PLEASURES OF READING.

sto-ries	fetched	trav-els
be-gan	en-joyed	read-ing

TOM liked ver-y much to hear sto-ries a-bout dogs and hor-ses, so he said, "I wish I could read like Will. I can-not make out the big words." Will said, "Well, if you will tell me when you come to a word that you can-not make out, I will help you."

So Tom sat down and be-gan to read a sto-ry a-bout a man who was lost in the snow and was found out by a dog, who fetched some men to him, and so saved his life. He did not find the book so hard as he thought it would be, and when he had read the sto-ry through, he said to Will, "That is a grand book. I have en-joyed my-self quite as much as if I had been play-ing. I should like to read some more of it."

"Very well," said Will, "you can have it an-y time you want it. I have oth-er books a-bout trades, and a-bout trav-els, and one a-bout Rob in Hood, and one a-bout poor boys who be-came great men."

"I did not know that there were books like that. I thought they were all a-bout things which I do not un-der-stand." "Oh, no," said Will, "most of my books are just what you would like. I have one all a-bout games, and rab-bits, and fish-ing."

From that time for-ward Tom grew ver-y fond of books. His teach-er could not make out how it was that he got on so well with

his read-ing.   The se-cret was that he
took a de-light in it, and used to read   ·
at home all the books he could get.

———o———

WHAT THE BIRDS SAY.

mer-ry   soar-ing   waste
ear-ly   spar-row   splen-dor

WHAT sings the mer-ry lark
In the blue sky,
Ris-ing so ear-ly,
And soar-ing so high?
"Get up, dear chil-dren,
Night-time has fled,
All GOOD boys and girls
Should be out of bed."
What does the spar-row chirp,
Look-ing for food,
All the day o-ver,
To feed its young brood?

" Dear lit-tle chil-dren,
   Waste not the day
Do not for-get
   That WORK sweet-ens play."

What sings the pret-ty bird,
   When in the west
Sink-eth the bright sun
   In splen-dor to rest?

" Dear lit-tle chil-dren,
  Day-light has fled,
All GOOD boys and girls
  Should now be in bed."

———o———

THE FARM HOUSE.

thatch   need-ed   flails
stacks   thresh   win-now

THIS is a farm-house. It has a
roof of thatch. There are stacks
of grain be-side it.

Men bring the grain when it is
cut down, and make it in-to stacks,
to keep it till it is need-ed.

Then they take it to the barn and
thresh the straw with flails, till the
grain falls out. Then they lift a-way
the straw, and win-now the grain
from the chaff.

A flail is a stout stick joined by a

thong to a han-dle. It thus plays free-ly on the straw, when the men thresh with it.

Can that be the farm-er cross-ing the bridge?

The wa-ter is rushing o-ver stones and rocks be-low. It must flow from the hills you see.

Rich farm-ers now use ma-chines in-stead of flails to thresh the grain.

ALL MUST WORK.

pa-pa	flow-er	hay-rick
mam-ma	hon-ey	him-self

THERE was a lit-tle boy, and his pa-pa and mam-ma sent him to school. It was a ver-y fine morn-ing; the sun shone, and the birds on the trees were sing-ing.

Now this lit-tle boy did not love his book, for he was a fool-ish lit-tle boy; and he had a wish to play and not go to school. He saw a bee fly-ing a-bout from flow-er to flow-er; so he said, "Pret-ty bee! will you come and play with me?" But the bee said, "No, I must not be i-dle; I must go and gath-er hon-ey." Then the lit-tle boy met a dog, and he said, "Dog! will you play with me?" But the dog said, "No, I must not be i-dle: I am go-ing to catch a hare for my mas-ter's din-ner. I must run and catch it."

Then the lit-tle boy went to a hay-rick, and he saw a bird pull-ing some hay out of the hay-rick, and he said, "Bird! will you come and play with me?" But the bird said, "No, I must not be i-dle; I must get some hay to make my nest with, and some moss, and some wool."

Then the lit-tle boy said to him-self, "What, is no one i-dle? then lit tle boys must not be i-dle."

So he went to school, and sat down to his les-son; and the mas-ter said he was a good boy.

———o———

THE BULL AND THE POST.

| mead-ow | fling | lan-tern |
| hoofs | fierce | gore |

A FARM-ER had a mead-ow in which he kept a bull.

In time the bull came to think the mead-ow his own, and would let no one cross it nor come near it if he could get at them. He would put down his head, tear up the grass with

his hoofs, fling up his tail, and rush
as though mad at an-y one who was
rash e-nough to try to cross the
mead-ow.

At last he grew so fierce and proud,
he would not let the farm-er come
near him. Then the farm-er thought

it was time to tame the bull, and to
teach him that he was not the lord
of the mead-ow, and must let peo-ple
go a-cross it when they chose.

So the farm-er got a stout post,
and, on a dark night, he went to the
mead-ow and put in the post, and
beat down the earth round it tight
and close.

Now this post had an i-ron ring in it, from which hung a heav-y chain. Then the farm-er went to the spot where the bull lay, and swung a lan-tern to and fro in front of the bull, so that the light went in his eyes. The bull got up, and rushed at the light to gore it. By this trick he was drawn to the post, and the farm-er put a strong rope round his neck, and tied him fast to the chain.

All night the bull lay still, but, as soon as day broke, he roared with rage to see how he had been caught. He ran at the post, to try to knock it down, but found it on-ly hurt his head. Then he tried to break the chain, but it would not snap, in spite of his jerks.

The bull soon saw it was of no use try-ing to break his bonds, so he gave up, and made up his mind to gore the farm-er when he came to set him free. But the farm-er, who knew how wick-ed the bull was, did not choose to let him loose, but he kept him tied up, and fed him well, and then sold him to a butch-er to be made in-to beef.

———o———

GOD WILL KNOW IT.

beg-gar   pen-ny   ac-count

way-side   pock-et   blind-ness

TWO chil-dren were one day out walk-ing, when they saw a poor old blind beg-gar, ver-y weak, sit-ting on a lit-tle stone by the way-side, with his hat rest-ing up-on his knees. His hair was white, and his face was pale and worn. On his breast he had a

card with these words on it, "Pi-ty
the poor Blind."

The lit-tle boy had a pen-ny in his

pock-et.   Pit-y-ing the poor old man,
he was a-bout to wake him to give
him the pen-ny, when his sis-ter stop-
ped him. "Do not wake him," she

said. "But who will tell him," said the lit-tle boy, "that I gave him my pen-ny?" "No one," said his sis-ter, "but God will know."

Ev-er-y thing that we do is seen by God; and we may be sure that he loves to see us do good and kind deeds. We ought not to seek for praise or e-ven thanks when we do a kind deed.

When we meet a blind man, we ought to show him great kind-ness, and lend him our eyes. I mean we ought to give him an-y help he may need on ac-count of his blind-ness.

———o———

"BITE BIGGER, BILLY."

| cit-y | taste | self-ish |
| dirt-y | greed-y | con-duct |

ONE day a man saw two boys go-ing a-long the streets of a

"OH, BILLY, IF HERE AIN'T HALF AN AP-PLE!"

large cit-y. Their feet were bare,
and their clothes were rag-ged and
dirt-y, and tied by pieces of string
One of the boys was quite hap-py
o-ver a bunch of with-ered flow-ers,
which he had just picked up in the
street. "I say, Bil-ly," said he to the
boy that was with him, "wasn't some
one real good to drop these flow-ers
just where I could find them? They're
so pret-ty and sweet! Look sharp,
Bil-ly, may-be you'll find some-thing
by and by."

In a short time the man heard the
boy's mer-ry voice a-gain, say-ing,—

"Oh, Bil-ly, here is half of an ap-
ple, and it is so clean! Though I
have found it, you may take first bite."

Bil-ly was go-ing to take a very lit-
tle taste of it, when his friend said,—

" Bite big-ger, Bil-ly, we may find some more be-fore long."

What a no-ble heart that poor boy had, in spite of his rags and dirt ! There was no one for him to be kind to but the poor rag-ged boy at his side. But he was show-ing him all the kind-ness in his pow-er when he said, " Bite big-ger, Billy." There was noth-ing greed-y, noth-ing self-ish a-bout that boy. His con-duct shows us how e-ven a poor beg-gar boy can do good by show-ing kind-ness.

———o———

A PRECIOUS PLANT.

| bas-ket | fret-ted | re-lief |
| grum-bled | joked | pa-tience |

TWO girls, Ma-ry and Fan-ny, were go-ing to the near-est town, each bear-ing on her arm a heav-y bas-ket of fruit to sell.

Mary grum-bled and fret-ted all

the way, but Fan-ny on-ly joked and laughed.

At last Ma-ry got out of all pa-

tience, and said in an an-gry tone.
" How can you go on laugh-ing so ?
Your bas-ket is as heav-y as mine,
and you are not one bit strong-er. I
don't know how it is."

"Oh," said Fan-ny, "it is ea-sy
e-nough to know. I have a cer-tain
lit-tle plant that I put un-der my
load, and it makes it so light I hard-
ly feel it. Why don't you do the
same?"

"In-deed!" said Ma-ry, "it must
be a ver-y prec-ious plant I wish
I could light-en my load with it.
Where does it grow? Tell me.
What do you call it?"

" It grows," re-plied Fan-ny, " in
an-y place where you plant it and
give it a chance to take root, and
there's no know-ing the re-lief it gives.
Its name is PA-TIENCE."

ALICE AND HER KITTENS.

poured   shelves   cream

kit-tens   feast   mice

I HAVE poured in-to the dish some sweet milk for you, you dear lit-tle kit-tens,—milk fresh from the cow.

There are five of you in all; but one hides be-hind the old moth-er cat, and seems a-fraid to come out. She keeps so far back in the dark, I have to look sharp to see her.

Now I will give each of you a name. Your moth-er's, you know, is Sly. I gave her that name, be-cause she used to hide be-hind a jar in the milk room, and not let us know she was there; and then, when we had gone out and shut the door, she would jump up-on the shelves, and have a feast of cream.

I hope you will not take af-ter your moth-er in all things, lit-tle kit-tens: she keeps a-way the mice, and she makes the dog a-fraid of her; but she is fond-er of cream than we like to , and she hunts the dear birds.

Well, now, you black kit-ten, you were the first to run to the plate; so I shall call you Greed-y.

Your black and white sis-ter I shall call Muff, be-cause her fur is so soft.

The kit-ten with the white nose I shall call Touch-me-not, be-cause she tried to scratch me when I took her up.

You weak lit-tle one, with your head all white, you seem al-most a-fraid to leave your moth-er's side; I shall call you La-zy-Bones, be-cause you spend most of your time in sleep.

As for you, lit-tle gray one, I shall call you Scam-per, be-cause you run and hide when you hear an-y one com-ing.

Now, lit-tle kit-tens, let me give you a word of ad-vice.

If you are good, and be-have your-selves, I will bring you up with great care, and find nice homes for you, as soon as you are old e-nough to be sent a-way from your moth-er.

THE LOST BOY.

foot-man   ale-house   fire-place
friend   lone-ly   bathe

A LONG time a-go, on the first of May, a grand din-ner used to be giv-en in the house of a rich man, in Lon-don, to the sweeps of that cit-y.   Would you like me to tell you how this came about?

The la-dy of this grand house had a lit-tle son, of whom she was ver-y fond.   She had gone with him, in the sum-mer, to a large house she had a-mong parks and woods.   The

THE LOST BOY.

lit-tle boy was sent for a walk, day by day, with the foot-man, who was told not to leave the boy out of his sight.

But a day came when the foot-man met an old friend, and was so fool-ish as to go in-to an ale-house with him to drink, let-ting the boy stand out-side. Af-ter stay-ing some time drink-ing he came out to take the child home, but there was no child to be seen.

The child's poor mam-ma was be-side her-self with grief at the loss of her boy. Men were sent out to all parts, far and near, in search of him, but all was of no use.

Month af-ter month flew by, and no news of her boy came to the poor la-dy. She would not, she could not, cheer her-self; but lived lone-ly and sad, in the great house in the park, from which the lost child had tak-en away all joy.

At last, a sis-ter of the la-dy was to wed a rich man in Lon-don, and the la-dy gave a grand ball in her town house, on the wed-ding-day. But just as they were sit-ting down to the sup-per ta-ble, a cry of "Fire!" a-rose. The cooks had up-set some fat in-to the grate, and set the flue on fire.

The sweeps were sent for, and a lit-tle boy was put in-to the flue to climb up and sweep down the soot. But the smoke well nigh choked the poor boy, and he fell in-to the fire-place. The la-dy be-ing told of this, came her-self to bathe his tem-ples and neck, and was do-ing so, when she gave a loud cry, " Oh, my boy!" and faint-ing, fell on the ground.

But she soon got well, and then threw her arms a-round the lit-tle sweep, and wept, for he was her long ost boy! She had seen a mark on his neck which told her he was her son.

The mas-ter sweep told the la-dy that he got the boy from a gyp-sy wo-man, who told him that he was her own son. The little boy had been sto-len by her, and sold to this man.

For joy at get-ting her son back, the la-dy gave a din-ner to all the sweeps in London, who chose to come, ev-er-y year on the first day of May; that be-ing the day on which her son was found.

E-ven to this day the sweeps of London make a hol-i-day of the first of May.

THE WHALE.

whale	girth	jel-ly
gills	fringe	blub-ber

THE whale is not a fish, yet it lives in the wide deep. If it were a

fish it would have gills, but it has lungs, like the beasts on dry land, and it comes up to the air for breath, which it draws in-to its lungs just as

we do. It is the big-gest of all liv-
ing things, for it is six-ty feet long,
or more, and its girth round the mid-
dle is ver-y huge. Its head is a quar-
ter, or e-ven a third of the whole
whale, and its tail is from twen-ty to
twen-ty five feet a-cross. Its eyes
are on the sides of its head, and they
are a-bout the size of the eyes of an
ox. It has no teeth, but a fringe of
whale-bone, in-stead, to strain its food
from the wa-ter. It lets the wa-ter
run out, the whale-bone keep-ing back
the lit-tle liv-ing specks of jel-ly on
which it lives. There are some-times
two tons of whale-bone in the mouth
of a whale. Its throat is ver-y small,
not be-ing more than an inch and a
half a-cross.

Its skin has a thick coat-ing of fat
or blub-ber on the under side, and

this fat weighs, in a large whale, more than thir-ty tons. It is from a foot to two feet thick. It keeps the whale warm, and makes it able to rise to the sur-face with l -tle ef-fort.

---o---

THE WHALE.

PART II.

swamp   har-poon   nois-y
hurls   a-fresh   bawl-ing

SHIPS go to the far North, where the whale is found, to get it for the oil in its fat, and for its whale-bone. When a whale is seen, boats put off af-ter it, but I should not like to be in them, for one dash of the whale's tail will swamp a boat, or toss its crew in-to the air. When the poor whale comes up for breath, the man in the bow of the boat next it hurls a har-poon, or i-ron dart, at it. There is a long rope at the end of the har-poon, and the men in the boat let this run out as fast as they can, when the whale is struck.

The barb of the dart no soon-er sinks in-to its flesh, than the whale swims off ver-y fast, or sinks far down in-to the deep, draw-ing the rope with it. The crews wait till it comes to the top for breath, and then more har-poons are hurled in-to it. It swims off and sinks a-gain, but when it ris-es, more har-poons still are stuck in-to it, till it is worn out, faints, floats on its back on the sur-face, and is soon dead. The crews haul their prey by the har-poon ropes to the ship's side.

The fat is now cut off and put in-to huge ket-tles to melt in-to train oil,

and a nois-y, dirt-y time it is: the
men sing-ing and bawl-ing at their
task, and the whole ship smell-ing ol
oil, which stains all the deck. If the
whales can be got, so that all the
casks the ship can hold are full of oil,
the ship sails home.

———o———

SAINT MARY, CALLED THE SINNER.

skull   pit-y   mon-ey
sin-ners   plen-ty   oint-ment

WHO is this la-dy, that looks so
sad? Why has she this skull
be-fore her?

My dear chil-dren, when you get
old-er, and are a-ble to stud-y all a-
bout the life of our Lord, you will
learn that Je-sus did all he could for
poor sin-ners. Ma-ry was one of the

ST. MARY, CALLED THE SINNER.

great-est sin-ners in the coun-try. But no one spoke an-y kind word to her, and she was go-ing on in her wild life, till one day she saw Je-sus. Our dear Lord was so kind ; he look-ed at her with so much pit-y that her poor heart, though full of ev-er-y sin, was at once touched. She said to her-self: "Well, here is one who will not drive me a-way." She had plen-ty of mon-ey, and went off to buy some cost-ly oint-ment. When she came back, she went in-to a house where Je-sus was sit-ting with many peo-ple. She nev-er looked at an-y-bod-y ex-cept Je-sus. She went straight up to him, and fell up-on her knees. She broke the box of fine oint-ment and let it drip on the feet of Je-sus, at the same time that her tears of sor-row fell in streams. She had no tow-el. But she took her long tress-es of hair and wiped the feet of our Lord with them. Je-sus was so much pleased that he said to her: " Mar-y, man-y sins are washed a-way from your soul for you love me so much."

She did pen-ance all the rest of her life. She al-ways thought of death, for she knew that if we of-ten think of death we will nev-er com-mit sin.

HUNTER AND THE LION.

fierce	watch-ing	waved
shag-gy	ledge	yells

THE lion is a brave and fierce beast. His limbs are ver-y strong, and he has a shag-gy mane and a long tail. His roar is ver-y loud and when heard at night it seems like dis-tant thun-der.

A hunt-er, in a far-off land, where li-ons are found, was on his way

home. He had to cross a field where he saw a li-on close by, watch-ing him. The hunt-er had lost his bul-lets, and he could not run a-way from the li-on so he looked a-bout for a safe place to hide for the night, but could see none.

At last he fell on a plan to cheat the li-on. He crept un-der the ledge of a high cliff. It was now dark, but the man could see that the li-on had come af-ter him, and was a lit-tle dis-tance off. He took off his hat and coat,and put-ting them on his gun, so as to make them look like a man, he waved them a-bove the edge of the rock.

As soon as the li-on came up, he saw the coat and the hat, and at once made a spring at them. He bound-ed right o-ver the cliff where the man lay, and was kill-ed on the rocks be-low.

EARLY RISING.

ris-ing   wealth-y   plough

rhyme   crow-ing   start-ed

A LL who wish to get on in the world should make a point of

ris-ing ev-er-y day with the sun. Those who take a walk in the fresh, cool, morn-ing air, are far more read-y for work than those who lie in bed till they have on-ly just time to dress and be off to school. We all know the rhyme—

" Ear-ly to bed and ear-ly to rise,
Makes a man health-y wealth-y and wise."

And if we would keep it in mind, we would be more health-y than we are, and more con-tent. The cock al-ways tells us when day is com-ing, and to man-y an i-dler his crow-ing must seem to mean some-thing like this:

" 'Up, up,' cries the wake-ful cock,
'Did you not hear the vil-lage clock?
I have been up for an hour or more,
Crow-ing a-loud while you still snore.
Dob-bin has gone with the boy to plough,
Bet-ty has start-ed to milk the cow.
Sure there is plen-ty for all to do,
And all are up, young friend, but you.'"

————o————

THE BEAR AND THE KETTLE.

| hun-gry | think-ing | squeeze |
| vil-lage | burnt | crush |

ONCE a bear was ver-y hun-gry. Not be-ing a-ble to find an-y

food in the woods, he came to a lit-tle
vil-lage, to see what he could find there.

The door of the first house that
he came to was o-pen; and peep-ing
in, he found that no one was at home.

In he went, and be-gan smell-ing
a-bout. But he could find no food.
At last he came to a ket-tle of boil-
ing wa-ter, which was by the side of
the fire.

Not know-ing what it was, and

think-ing that there might be some-thing good in-side, he smelt the ket-tle, and in so do-ing burnt his nose.

This made him ver-y an-gry with the ket-tle. So he said : " I will pun-ish you for burn-ing my nose ; " and he took the ket-tle up in his fore-paws and tried hard to crush it a-gainst his breast.

The more he squeezed it, the more he burnt him-self, and the more an-gry he grew. He roared with pain. At last he was forced to drop the ket-tle, and, in so do-ing, scald-ed him-self with the hot wa-ter.

The noise which he made brought some men to the spot to see what was the cause of it. Look-ing through the win-dow they could see the bear danc-ing a-bout in great pain. They then got their guns and shot him.

In that land, if a man hurts him-self when he tries to hurt some-body else, the peo-ple still say, " He is like the bear and the ket-tle."

———o———

GOING AN ERRAND.

cot-tage   wid-ow   nut-megs
coun-try   poul-try   cur-rants

MRS. Smith lives in a ver-y pret-ty lit-tle rose-cov-ered cot-tage in the coun-try.   It is some dis-tance from the near-est vil-lage, and she is not a-ble to walk so far her-self.   She would of-ten be at a loss to know how to pro-cure man-y things she wants in the house if it were not for her on-ly son Mar-tin.   He is al-ways read-y and will-ing, when not at school, to help his moth-er who is a wid-ow and in bad health.   It is

he who keeps the gar-den in such

nice or-der, and sees that the pigs,
cow, and poul-try have plen-ty to eat

and drink, and clean sheds to sleep in at night. In the pict-ure we see him just go-ing out on an er-rand. His moth-er is tell-ing him to be sure and not for-get that she wants a pound of tea and some su-gar, be-sides rice, nut-megs, and cur-rants, and to be ver-y care-ful with the mon-ey which she has tied up in a cor-ner of the bag he holds in his hand. Mar-tin prom-is-es not to for-get what he is told, and not to lose the mon-ey or drop an-y of the par-cels on his road home. And on the way he will go for a mo-ment in-to the vil-lage church, to ask our dear Lord to bless his good moth-er. Let us hope that she will long be spared to him.

THE CLOUDS.

wan-der   sun-shine   bear-ers
dark-ness won-der   flow-ers

" CLOUDS that wan-der through
          the sky,
Some-times low and some-times high;
In the dark-ness and the night,
In the sun-shine warm and bright:
Ah! I won-der much if you
Have got an-y work to do?"
" Yes, we're bus-y night and day,
As o'er the earth we take our way;
We are bear-ers of the rain
To the grass, and flow-ers, and grain.
When you coast-ing wish to go,
But for us you'd have no snow,
And when skies are warm and blue,
We shade the bright, hot sun from
          you. "

TREES.

trunk roots win-ter

branch-es breathes blos-soms

THE bod-y of a tree is called its trunk. From the trunk spread out its branch-es. They shoot up in-to the air; and there are al-so man-y branch-es be-low, which shoot down in-to the ground. The branch-es which shoot in-to the ground are called roots.

The skin of a tree is called its bark. If we were to strip off the bark the tree would not live.

A tree draws sap from the earth through its roots. If we were to cut the roots, the tree would die. A tree eats and drinks with its roots; and breathes through its leaves.

In win-ter most trees lose all their leaves; but their branch-es are dotted all o-ver with lit-tle buds. When the warm sun comes in spring, these buds swell and o-pen out and burst; and the leaves come out of them.

A tree has al-so blos-soms. If the tree is a fruit tree, the blos-soms grow in-to ap-ples, or pears, or plums. If the tree is a nut-tree, then the blos-soms grow in-to ha-zel-nuts, or beech-nuts, or chest-nuts.

Some trees nev-er shed their leaves; they change them slow-ly, but nev-er all at once. Thus, the pine-tree and the ce-dar-tree do not lose their leaves in win-ter, and are called ev-er-greens.

Who is it that makes the trees do these things?

It is God. Don't you know that God can do all things, and that he does all these things in this world for us? We should be ver-y thankful to God for his great kind-ness to us.

———o———

READY WIT.

chim-ney   wors-ted   stock-ing
foun-dry   pul-ley   keep-sake

A F-TER hard toil for man-y weeks, the tall chim-ney of a new foun-dry was built. The men put the last stroke to their work, and came down as fast as they could. In his haste, the last but one drew the rope out of the pul-ley.

They saw one man left at the top, with no means to come down. What could be done? There was no scaf-fold, and no lad-der would reach half the height.

They all stood in si-lence to look up at their lone-ly friend on the top.

Just then his wife came by, and, with quick thought and good sense, she was a-ble to save her hus-band.

"John," she called out with all her strength, "rove your stock-ing; be-gin at the toe." He knew at once what she meant, and draw-ing off his stock-ing—no doubt knit by his wife —cut off the end, and soon set free the thread. He roved a long piece, and to this he tied a lit-tle bit of brick, and gent-ly let it down for ea-ger hands to reach.

Mean-time his wife had brought a ball of small twine, which was made fast to the wors-ted. With a shout, they told John to pull up a-gain. He did so, and they heard the words, "I have it." The pul-ley rope was then made fast to the twine.

With a glad heart John drew it up,

put it o-ver the pul-ley; and tak-ing
up the rest of the stock-ing, which was
to him a keep-sake for life, he let him-
self down as the oth-er men had done,
till he reached the ground in safe-ty.

———o———

JESUS TAKEN DOWN FROM THE CROSS.

birth   crowned   con-sole
lis-ten   lad-der   pray-er

WHAT a good thing it is to
know how to read! We can
learn all a-bout the birth, life and
death of our dear Lord.

Here we see Je-sus ta-ken down
from the cross. Some of his friends
have asked leave from Pi-late to take
down the bod-y. Look! the head is
crowned with thorns. The arms are
stiff and cold. Who is this sad la-dy

JESUS TAKEN DOWN FROM THE CROSS.

at the feet of Je-sus? She is his moth-er, Ma-ry. Would you not like to help to con-sole Ma-ry? Do you want to know how you can make her glad? Oh yes, teach-er, we all want to know this. Well, lis-ten, my dear chil-dren. To make Ma-ry, the moth-er of Je-sus, hap-py, nev-er com-mit sin. Strive to please her Son, by do-ing what he com-mands. Ev-er-y time you com-mit sin you nail Je-sus to the cross. When you be-come sor-ry, you take him down a-gain.

Who is the wo-man on the oth-er side of the lad-der? That is Ma-ry, called the Sin-ner, be-cause she was once so bad. But, dur-ing his preach-ing, Je-sus brought her back to God's love.

No mat-ter how bad a per-son

may be, Je-sus will al-ways re-ceive him a-gain if he comes back to him.

Where will Je-sus be placed when tak-en down from the cross? He will be placed in the arms of Ma-ry, his moth-er. Now let us say a lit-tle pray-er, that when we die we may al-so fall in-to the arms of Ma-ry, Queen of heav-en, and moth-er of all good chil-dren.

THE INFANT JESUS IN THE TEMPLE.

A lit-tle child to God was brought,
　　Sin-less and not de-filed :
Pur-er than any spot-less lamb—
　　Who was that lit-tle child?

He wept and smiled, and played as we,
　　And yet from Heav-en He came :

He was the Ho-ly Son of God,
  And Je-sus was His name.

O Sav-iour dear! O sin-less Babe!
  As Thou wert like to me,
May I, in ev-er-y ho-ly thing,
  Grow al-so like to Thee!

———o———

THE WILD DUCK.

YOU must be ver-y qui-et if you wish to see the ducks in the wa-ter, for they are ver-y tim-id and ver-y watch-ful. We must get near e-nough to no-tice how pret-ty the drakes are. Dur-ing the shoot-ing sea-son the drake wears his fin-est feath-ers. His head is glos-sy, and about his neck he wears a white ring like a col-lar. The four mid-dle feath-ers of his tail are black, and curl over

in an odd lit-tle tuft. The oth-er
feath-ers are gray-ish brown, edged
with white. His wings have two
white bars a-cross them.

The duck is not so gay a bird.
Her feath-ers are all brown, of man-y

shades. In the sum-mer, the drake
los-es his bright plum-age, and has on-
ly a so-ber brown coat like the duck.

If the least noise is made, the old
birds give a warn-ing, and all fly a-
way.

WHAT GOOD A CHILD CAN DO.

A lit-tle child I am in-deed
    And lit-tle do I know:
Much help and care I yet shall need,
    That I may wis-er grow,
If I would ev-er hope to do
    Things great and good, and use-
    ful too.

But ev-en now I ought to try
    To do what good I may:
God nev-er meant that such as I
    Should on-ly live to play
And talk and laugh, and eat and
    drink
    And sleep and wake, and nev-er
    think.

I may, if I but have the mind,
    Do good in man-y ways;

Plen-ty to do the young may find
 In these our bus-y days;

Sad would it be, though young and
 small,
 If I were of no use at all.

Then let me try each day and hour
  To act up-on this plan;
What lit-tle good is in my pow-er,
  To do it while I can.
If to be use-ful thus I try,
  I may do bet-ter by-and-by.

EVERY LITTLE BOY'S FRIEND.

WHOSE like-ness is this? Can an-y lit-tle boy tell me? It is the pic-ture of the ho-ly man who was the first Broth-er of the Chris-tian Schools. He was born a-bout two hun-dred and for-ty years a-go. His pa-rents were ver-y wealth-y, and he be-came a priest. When he saw so man-y lit-tle boys who nev-er went to school, he said he would

teach them him-self, and get oth-ers to help him. His name was John Bap-tist De La Salle. You should love this good man dear-ly. Hon-or his mem-o-ry. Ask him to make you as good as the lit-tle boys he taught, two hun-dred years a-go. How do you know? Per-haps God wants you to teach lit-tle boys when you grow up and be-come men. That would in-deed be a great fa-vor be-stowed up-on you. Ask your teach-er to tell you all a-bout the ho-ly man who taught lit-tle chil-dren to know and love God.

———o———

"I WOULD KEEP ON PLAYING."

SOME peo-ple have wrong i-de-as about God. They think he is

ver-y cross, and nev-er wish-es chil-
dren to laugh, or play or be mer-ry.

This is all a mis-take. The on-ly
thing Al-might-y God wish-es us to
a-void is sin, and all that leads to

it. He has made the coun-try so
beau-ti-ful and fresh for us to walk in;
the riv-ers are so pure, the sea so
proud and great, for our use and ben-
e-fit. But when you stud-y at home
or in school, when you play in the
fields, fly your kite, try to beat your
friends at mar-bles, or any-thing else,
do ev-er-y-thing for God's sake. He
is so good that he will re-ward you,
e-ven for play-ing, just as a ten-der
pa-rent smiles on a sick-ly child when
tak-ing a heart-y meal.

One day, when a dear young Saint
was play-ing a game of ball, some
one asked his part-ners what they
would do, if told they would die in
half an hour. Some said they would
fall on their knees, right then and
there; oth-ers re-plied that they would
run to the Church. But, said an old

priest, what would you do, my lit-tle friend.? as he spoke to the young Saint. Well, an-swered the youth-ful play-er, I would fin-ish the game. This is my time for play; I be-gan af-ter of-fer-ing the game to God, I will con-tin-ue it for his sake.

You must act in like man-ner. Wheth-er you eat, or drink, or what-so-ev-er else you do, do all for the glo-ry of God.

WHAT LITTLE BOYS CAN DO.

PEO-PLE of-ten say " he is on-ly a lit-tle boy and can-not do any-thing." Do you be-lieve this? I hope not; for boys e-ven when quite young can do man-y use-ful things. They can make moth-er's heart rejoice by be-ing kind to small-er broth-ers or sis-ters. Lit-tle boys can say their pray-ers just as well as grown-up peo-ple. They can run er-rands,

help to keep the house ti-dy, read at night for moth-er and fa-ther, speak kind-ly to the ser-vants and car-ry food to the poor.

When ho-ly Da-vid was but a small boy he watched his fa-ther's flocks; Sam-u-el when a mere child, lived and prayed in the tem-ple; the most bless-ed vir-gin Ma-ry, the moth-er of God, went to the tem-ple when she was four or five years old; and Je-sus when a child, helped his fos-ter fa-ther Saint Jo-seph, in a car-pen-ter's shop. If lit-tle boys and girls could do noth-ing else than make their pa-pas and mam-mas hap-py, by be-ing gen-tle, kind and o-blig-ing, this would be a great thing in-deed When you think that moth-er has a head-ache, or is tired, ask her if you can do any-thing for her. Do not be a-shamed to help her at an-y kind of work. Bad boys may laugh at you, but this must not give you an-y trou-ble. A lit-tle boy who helps his moth-er to make a fire or who minds the ba-by while she is cook-ing sup-per, is do-ing just as much as a big man could do.

When-ev-er you have a chance, try to be of ser-vice at home. When you get back from school, ask moth-er if you can do any-thing for her. Per-haps she will not kiss you each time you of-fer to work for her, but you may be sure she will be ver-y much pleased.

Now, we are all go-ing to try how man-y things lit-tle boys can do. This will make fa-ther and moth-er proud of us. We will be the pride and the joy of our homes. God will bless us on earth, and af-ter a while, will call us to a hap-py land, where fa-ther and moth-er, broth-ers and sis-ters will be for-ev-er to-geth-er.

THE SACRED HEART.

PEACE, be still! Our God is
    dwell-ing
Si-lent on His al-tar throne;
Let us kneel, our bos-oms swell-ing
    With a joy but sel-dom known.
Heart of Je-sus! come we hith-er,
    With our bur-den, sad, with-in,
From a world, where chil-dren, fall-
    ing,
    Learn how hard it is to win,
In the bat-tle with that Ser-pent
    That our ru-in seeks, by sin.
Sa-cred Heart, be our pro-tec-tion,
    Lead us past the thorn-y way,
Take us to the bet-ter land, where

THE ORPHAN.

dais-ies   search   through

MY fa-ther and moth-er are dead,
Nor friend, no rre-la-tion I know;

And now the cold earth is their bed,
And dais-ies will over them grow.

cast my eyes into the tomb,
  The sight made me bit-ter-ly cry;
I said, "And is this the dark room,
  Where my fa-ther and moth-er
    must lie!"

I cast my eyes round me a-gain,
  In hopes some pro-tec-tor to see;
Alas! but the search was in vain,
  For none had com-pas-sion on me.

I cast my eyes up to the sky,
  I groan'd, though I said not a word;
Yet God was not deaf to my sigh,
  The Friend of the fa-ther-less heard;

And since I have trust-ed his care,
  And learn'd on his word to de-pend,
He has kept me from ev-e-ry snare,
  And been my true Fa-ther and
    Friend.

ST. JOHN THE BAPTIST.

priv-i-lege   pen-ance   faith-ful

HOW would you like to be spe-
cial-ly prais-ed by our di-vine
Lord him-self? How pleas-ed you
would be! And your par-ents and
friends! Yet, such was the rare priv-i-
lege of St. John the Bap-tist. He was
the pre-cur-sor or fore-run-ner of
our bles-sed Sav-iour. Some time
be-fore the ap-pear-ance of Je-sus
Christ as a Teach-er, St. John had
gone all through the coun-try a-
round the Jor-dan, tell-ing the peo-
ple to do pen-ance, for the king-dom
of heav-en was at hand. By this St.
John meant that he who was to
o-pen the gates of heav-en by his death
was soon to ap-pear.

Af-ter preach-ing for some time,
St. John was cast in-to pris-on. You

must know that the Bap-tist was a ver-y brave man, and he was not a-fraid to tell King Her-od that he would be pun-ish-ed by God un-less he gave up his e-vil ways. For this just re-proach, St. John was cast in-to the pub-lic pris-on. While there, he heard of the preach-ing of Je-sus, and sent two friends to see the Mes-siah. When they came to Je-sus he spoke of St. John, and said he was the great-est per-son who was ever born of wom-an.

St. John had ear-ly shown him-self to be a child of grace. His youth was spent in the des-ert where he lived a ver-y aus-tere life. His food was a sort of large in-sect call-ed a lo-cust, some-thing like our grass-hop-per, and for drink he took wild hon-ey or pure wa-ter.

St. John preach-ed pen-ance to the peo-ple. We too must do pen-

ance, or we will all per-ish. Our Sav-
iour tells us so him-self. If we do pen-
ance, and live as good Chris-tians,
we too will one day be prais-ed by
Je-sus Christ. He will say to us,
Come, good and faith-ful ser-vant,
en-ter in-to the joy of the Lord.
Then we will meet St. John the
Bap-tist, St. Jo-seph, the Apos-tles,
our bless-ed Lady, and all those who
were with Je-sus Christ, and help-ed
him dur-ing his three and thir-ty
years' mis-sion, dur-ing which time
he went a-bout ev-ery-where, "do-ing
good." What a hap-py, joy-ful day
that will be!

SPEAK THE TRUTH.

IF you have a truth to say,
  Speak it al-ways, come what may;

Say it firm-ly, do not fear,
  False-hood flies when truth is near.
When vile slan-der walks a-broad,
  Helped by trick-er-y and fraud,

He who fears to speak his mind,
  Is nei-ther friend-ly, brave, nor
    kind.
Speak the truth, and take the risk—
  Truth is re-al, truth is strong;
It is cer-tain that a lie
  Will soon ex-pire; truth can-not
    die.
Oh! how sad it is to see
  How pale, con-fused that boy
    must be
Who, ly-ing, los-es friends be-low,
  And risks to live in end-less woe